M000120619

GHOUL BROTHERS

The Caravanserai Stories

TAHIR SHAH

ANCA CHELARU

GHOUL BROTHERS

The Caravanserai Stories

TAHIR SHAH

ANCA CHELARU

MMXXII

Secretum Mundi Publishing Ltd
124 City Road
London
EC1V 2NX
United Kingdom

www.secretum-mundi.com
info@secretum-mundi.com

First published as a limited edition by Secretum Mundi Publishing Ltd, 2021
Published in this edition, 2022

GHOUL BROTHERS

© TAHIR SHAH

Artwork drawn by Anca Chelaru

Tahir Shah asserts the right to be identified as the Author of the Work
in accordance with the Copyright, Designs and Patents Act 1988.

A CIP catalogue record for this title is available from the British Library.

VERSION: 12012023

Visit the author's website:
Tahirshah.com

ISBN 978-1-914960-55-0

For Tom, Yoshi, and Sebastian,
with love

Eight strangers were clustered around the campfire of the caravanserai – silhouetted, ragged, and ripened by adventure. As the flames licked the darkness, sparks spitting up into the nocturnal firmament, the traveller dressed in indigo cleared his throat and told his tale...

The sixth son of the sixth son, I was raised in a family blessed with good health and fine fortune.

My brothers and I had splendid clothing to wear, delicious food to eat, and were educated by private tutors. There was, however, a certain misfortune of which no one ever spoke.

Unlike me, or our parents,
all five of my brothers were ghouls.

As I had never known siblings any different,
I was happy enough with the ones I had. It was
only as I grew from infancy into adolescence that
I came to see they were unusual.

In day-to-day life, something else stood out about them more than the fact they were ghouls. You see, each one was deficient in one of the five senses.

The oldest, Gorem, was blind.
The next, Sorem, was deaf.

Then there was Korem, who had no sense of smell.
After him came Porem, who couldn't feel.
And lastly, Dorem, whose mouth didn't taste.

Being the youngest, I would play tricks on them
all – delighting in the mischief I caused.
Despite me causing trouble for them all,
each one appeared to love me.

On the night of the brightest harvest moon I can remember, my ghoul brothers lined up in the great hall of our family home. One by one they announced they'd fallen in love.

Our parents were effusive with their congratulations and asked whether the brides-to-be had accepted.

'I have not asked her yet,' said Gorem.
'Neither have I,' said Sorem.
'Nor I,' said Korem.
'Me neither,' said Porem.
'Nor I,' said Dorem.

Our father stepped forwards and cleared his throat.
'Well, at least tell me the names
of the lucky women,' he said.

'Her name is Amberine,' said Gorem.
'Her name is Amberine,' said Sorem.
'Her name is Amberine,' said Korem.
'Her name is Amberine,' said Porem.
'Her name is Amberine,' said Dorem.

Stepping forwards, our mother let out a shriek.
'Surely, each of the five brides-to-be are
not named Amberine?!' she exclaimed.

With a sigh, I stepped forwards.
'Dearest Mother and Father,' I said, 'all five of
them have fallen in love with the same girl.'

Our parents conferred for a good long time.
Then, both at once, they asked:
'And what of Amberine – whom does she love?'

The ghoul brothers flinched.
'We don't know,' they said in time with one another.

Again, our parents conferred. When they'd
discussed the matter long and hard,
our father turned to me:
'Go to Amberine,' he said, 'and enquire gently
whether she might grace us with her presence.'

The next evening, the potential bride ventured to our home, her brother as chaperone. The fact that all five of my ghoul brothers were in love with her was explained by my father. And the fact that she was not expected to even like any of them was explained by my mother.

A glint in her eye, Amberine stepped
forwards to where all five of my siblings
were lined up in order of age.
'I will marry the one who brings me
the object of my dreams.'

'What is the object of your dreams?'
the brothers asked.
'It's the one thing that touches all the senses,'
she said.

The information was relayed to Sorem in sign language, while the others wondered aloud what such an object could be.

One by one, my ghoul brothers vowed not to return without the object of Amberine's dreams, and left on their adventures.

I went to bed in the most silent house in existence. Never once, through a long and crowded childhood, had I imagined our home could be so quiet as it was on that night.

When morning eventually came, I found my
parents sitting on the balcony.
My mother rolled her eyes.
'Oh, what young men will do for the
want of a woman,' she said.
'I wonder which of them shall
win her hand,' my father added.

'I think I know the answer,' I said.

A week slipped by, in which the house seemed quieter with every minute that passed.

Then, a month came and went.

And before we knew it, an entire year had elapsed.

As the full moon rose up over the fields,
the silhouettes of five figures were spotted
streaming in from all directions of the compass.
Running to the window, I watched as
they entered one by one.

First came Gorem.
After him, Sorem.
Korem was next.
Then Porem.
And close behind was Dorem.
While they rested, a message was sent to Amberine.

She arrived at noon the next day,
her brother as chaperone once again.
On one side of the hall, Amberine, her brother,
my parents, and I took places on low divans.

Across from us,
my five ghoul brothers stood to attention.
When invited to do so, each one told the tale of his
journey, before revealing what he imagined to be
the object of Amberine's dreams.

As ever, Gorem went first:
'I may be blind, but my inability to see is the reason
I'll win the hand of my lovely bride-to-be,' he said.
'Unlike my brothers standing beside me, I am not
hindered by the follies besetting those
born with sight.

'As such, I was able to hone my other senses
on the adventure, and to perceive the
true nature of the quest.

'I travelled east, along the snaking river, through a succession of dominions and kingdoms. Guided by the kindness of strangers and by a burning zeal to succeed, I followed a long, twisting trail of clues.

'For weeks and months I wandered, until at last
I came to a forest as thick as any other in the
Kingdom of Unfortunate Salvation. An informant
there had revealed that a jinn, residing
in the trees, could answer any question posed
by a troubled mind.

'And he was right. For, as I was to discover, the most terrible creature imaginable existed there. He would surely have devoured me. But, thinking fast, I begged forgiveness for trespassing, and recounted to him the story of my journey – a tale of the truest affection.'

Gorem stepped towards the divan upon
which Amberine was reclining.
'From that wretched forest in the Kingdom of
Unfortunate Salvation, I have brought the object
of your dreams – the one thing that
touches all the senses.'

Her interest piqued, Amberine forced a smile.
As she did so, Gorem held up an ordinary acorn.

'I am sorry to tell you, that is not
the object of my dreams,' said Amberine.

The second of my ghoul brothers,
Sorem, went next.
'I may be deaf, but my inability to hear is the
reason I'll win the hand of my lovely bride-to-be,'
he said. 'Unlike my brothers standing beside me,
I am not hindered by the follies besetting
those born with hearing.

'As such, I was able to hone my other senses
on the adventure, and to perceive
the true nature of the quest.

'I travelled west, along the snaking river, through a succession of dominions and kingdoms. Guided by the kindness of strangers and by a burning zeal to succeed, I followed a long, twisting trail of clues.

'For weeks and months I wandered, until at last I came to a mountain as towering as any other in the Kingdom of Glorious Redemption. An informant there had revealed that a jinn, residing on an uppermost slope, could answer any question posed by a troubled mind.

'And he was right. For, as I was to discover, the most terrible creature imaginable existed there. He would have surely devoured me. But, thinking fast, I begged forgiveness for trespassing, and recounted to him the story of my journey –
a tale of the truest affection.'

Sorem stepped towards the divan upon
which Amberine was reclining.
'From that wretched slope in the Kingdom of
Glorious Redemption, I have brought the object of
your dreams – the one thing that
touches all the senses.'

Her interest piqued, Amberine forced a smile.
As she did so, Sorem held up an ordinary pebble.

'I am sorry to tell you, that is not the object of my dreams,' said Amberine.

My third ghoul brother, Korem, went next.
'I may not have the power of smell, but the lack of an olfactory nerve is the reason I'll win the hand of my lovely bride-to-be,' he said. 'Unlike my brothers standing beside me, I am not hindered by the follies besetting those born with a sense of smell.

'As such, I was able to hone my other senses on the adventure, and to perceive the true nature of the quest.

'I travelled south, along the snaking river, through a succession of dominions and kingdoms. Guided by the kindness of strangers and by a burning zeal to succeed, I followed a long, twisting trail of clues.

'For weeks and months I wandered, until at last I came to a desert as wide as any other in the Kingdom of Darkest Firmament. An informant there had revealed that a jinn, residing at a small oasis in the centre of the vast wilderness, could answer any question posed by a troubled mind.

'And he was right. For, as I was to discover,
the most terrible creature imaginable existed there.
He would have surely devoured me. But, thinking
fast, I begged forgiveness for trespassing, and
recounted to him the story of my journey –
a tale of the truest affection.'

Korem stepped towards the divan upon which
Amberine was reclining.
'From that fearful desert in the Kingdom of Darkest
Firmament, I have brought the object of your
dreams – the one thing that touches all the senses.'

Her interest piqued, Amberine forced a smile.
As she did so, Korem held up a handful of sand.

'I am sorry to tell you, that is not
the object of my dreams,' said Amberine.

The fourth of my ghoul brothers,
Porem, went next.
'I may not have a sense of touch, but my inability
to feel is the reason I believe I shall win the hand of
my lovely bride-to-be,' he said. 'Unlike my brothers
standing beside me, I am not hindered by the
follies besetting those born with feeling.

'As such, I was able to hone my other senses
on the adventure, and to perceive
the true nature of the quest.

'I travelled north, along the snaking river, through a succession of dominions and kingdoms. Guided by the kindness of strangers and by a burning zeal to succeed, I followed a long, twisting trail of clues.

'For weeks and months I wandered,
until at last I came to an inland sea in the Kingdom
of Slaked Thirst. An informant there had revealed
that a jinn, residing on an island in the middle
of the sea, could answer any question
posed by a troubled mind.

'And he was right. For, as I was to discover,
the most terrible creature imaginable existed there.
He would have surely devoured me. But, thinking
fast, I begged forgiveness for trespassing,
and recounted to him the story of my journey –
a tale of the truest affection.'

Sorem stepped towards the divan upon
which Amberine was reclining.
'From that wretched island in the Kingdom of
Slaked Thirst, I have brought the object of your
dreams – the one thing that touches all the senses.'

Her interest piqued, Amberine forced a smile.
As she did so, Porem held up a coconut.

'I am sorry to tell you, that is not
the object of my dreams,' said Amberine.

The fifth of my ghoul brothers, Dorem, went last. 'I may be unable to taste, but my inability to do so is the reason I believe I shall win the hand of my lovely bride-to-be,' he said. 'Unlike my brothers standing beside me, I am not hindered by the follies besetting those born with taste.

'As such, I was able to hone my other senses
on the adventure, and to perceive
the true nature of the quest.

'I travelled south-east, along the snaking river, through a succession of dominions and kingdoms. Guided by the kindness of strangers and by a burning zeal to succeed, I followed a long, twisting trail of clues.

'For weeks and months I wandered, until at last I came to an ocean as endless as any other between the Kingdom of Insufferable Damnation and eternity. An informant there had revealed that a jinn, residing in the ocean, could answer any question posed by a troubled mind.

'And he was right. For, as I was to discover,
the most terrible creature imaginable existed there.
He would have surely devoured me. But, thinking
fast, I begged forgiveness for trespassing,
and recounted to him the story of my journey –
a tale of the truest affection.'

Dorem stepped towards the divan upon
which Amberine was reclining.
'From that wretched ocean in the Kingdom of
Insufferable Damnation, I have brought
the object of your dreams – the one thing that
touches all the senses.'

Her interest piqued, Amberine forced a smile.
As she did so, Dorem held up a phial
filled with sea water.

'I am sorry to tell you, that is not
the object of my dreams,' said Amberine.

Once all five of my ghoul siblings had spoken, my father and mother rose to their feet. They both seemed a little embarrassed that their five sons had been unable to win the heart of the woman they all so adored.

Just before the assembly was adjourned,
I stood up and knelt before Amberine.

'I am the youngest of the brothers,' I said, 'and I confess that I have neither embarked on a journey, nor returned from one. But, despite the lack of miles to have passed beneath my feet, I believe I know the object of your dreams.'

Her interest piqued, Amberine forced a smile,
as she had already done five times.
'I think we have taken enough of the
young lady's time,' my father said curtly.
'She's surely tired of this game,' my mother added.

But, sitting up, Amberine held out
a delicate hand of invitation.
'All five of your siblings have regaled us with
their tales,' she said, 'and so it is only fair that you
should have a turn to speak.'

Still kneeling, and giving thanks,
I expressed my mind.
'I believe I know that the object of your dreams –
the one thing that touches all the senses –
is true love.'

Hearing the words, Amberine gasped,
her eyes welling with tears.
'You may not be ripened by adventure,' she said,
'but you are the only man in the world
I would ever wish to marry.'

And so, that's how I was matched with the most wonderful woman in all the world.

Finis

About the Author

Descended from a long line of storytellers, writers, and savants, Tahir Shah is one of the most prolific authors of his generation. He has published more than sixty books in numerous genres, including travel, fiction, and fantasy, as well as tales for children.

Raised in the tradition of Eastern 'teaching stories', Shah is passionate about stories and storytelling. He regards the ability to learn from folklore as being in us all, what he calls a 'default setting of humankind'. As well as having written scores of books, Shah has made documentaries for National Geographic TV and The History Channel. He is the founder and CEO of the charity, The Scheherazade Foundation.

About the Artist

Anca Chelaru grew up in a small town in Romania, where she picked up a passion for art and stories from her family's extensive library. She studied at the Ion Mincu University of Architecture and Urban Planning in Bucharest, and soon began pursuing her interest in book illustration – with a particular interest in fantasy and the surreal. Her main sources of artistic inspiration are the art nouveau movement and the post-war Romanian illustrators.

A REQUEST

If you enjoyed this book, please review it on your favourite online retailer or review website.

Reviews are an author's best friend.

To stay in touch with Tahir Shah, and to hear about his upcoming releases before anyone else, please sign up for his mailing list:

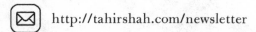 http://tahirshah.com/newsletter

And to follow him on social media, please go to any of the following links:

http://www.twitter.com/humanstew

@tahirshah999

http://www.facebook.com/TahirShahAuthor

http://www.youtube.com/user/tahirshah999

http://www.pinterest.com/tahirshah

https://www.goodreads.com/tahirshahauthor

http://www.tahirshah.com